Best of Flying Island
2014

INwords

Best of Flying Island 2014

Barbara Shoup, Executive Editor
David M. Hassler, Managing and Fiction Editor
J.L. Kato, Poetry Editor
Julianna Thibodeaux, Creative Nonfiction Editor

Michael Baumann, and Andrea Boucher, Copyeditors

Michael Baumann, Book Design and Layout

Andrea and Anna Boucher, Cover Design

INwords PUBLICATIONS
PRESENTED BY THE **INDIANA WRITERS CENTER**

Published by INwords: Indianapolis, IN
ISBN: 978-0-9849501-6-4

Best of Flying Island 2014

Edited by Barbara Shoup, David M. Hassler,
J.L. Kato, and Julianna Thibodeaux

INwords Publications
PO Box 30407
Indianapolis, IN 46230-0407

INDIANA WRITERS CENTER
BE A WRITER

WITH SUPPORT FROM:
ARTSCOUNCIL
AND THE CITY OF INDIANAPOLIS

Indiana Arts Commission
Connecting People to the Arts
This activity is made possible, in part, with support
from the Indiana Arts Commission and the National
Endowment for the Arts, a federal agency.

CONTENTS

FICTION

CREATIVE NONFICTION

INTRODUCTION

Back in 2002, a "final issue" of *The Flying Island* was published, bringing to an end a run of nine years of semi-annual issues filled with words from so many of our local and Midwestern writers. At that time, the Writers Center had decided to shift gears and publish a new, slicker, more ambitious annual magazine called *Maize*.

Unfortunately, *Maize* may have been a bit too ambitious—and it was certainly far too costly—so we managed only two editions. There followed a hiatus when the Writers Center didn't publish any of our local writers for a few years. Then, following a survey of our members, we were delighted to see that a considerable number wanted to see a return of the venerable *Flying Island.*

So, in 2007 and 2008, we published a pair of annual editions of the "new" *Flying Island,* showcasing more writing from familiar names in the Indiana writing community along with some new voices from around the Midwest. The response to both the content and the design was positive, but alas, again, the onset of recession and the scourge of economics proved too high a hurdle, so the publication went into hibernation again.

Five years later, though, in late 2013, we determined once again to lift the *Island* off the ground, thanks in large measure to modern technology! First off, we elected to go online and even make the publication an ongoing, blog-style work, with new pieces presented on a rolling basis weekly or more frequently through the year.

Second, we raised the needed funds through online crowdsourcing, with many of our members and supporters contributing what they could. We were delighted with the response and are grateful to everyone who chipped in to help us launch our third version of *Flying Island.*

During 2014, we published online just over fifty percent of the submissions we received—several with some editorial suggestions—with many from writers notching their first publishing credit. Our mission continues to be seeking great writing from Indiana authors—and those with strong ties to the state—and giving voice to our heritage and vision. So, we encourage everyone to send us your words and help carry on our Indiana literary tradition.

We hope you've enjoyed reading the poetry, fiction, and creative nonfiction online for our first year, and we're now proud to present our first annual *Best of Flying Island* for 2014. Many thanks to all the writers who shared their words with us, and also to J L Kato, our Poetry Editor; Julianna Thibodeaux, our Creative Nonfiction Editor; and of course to Barb Shoup, the Executive Director of the Indiana Writers Center and our Executive Editor. Congratulations to the select group of writers we are including in our first annual *Best of Flying Island.* We hope you enjoy this year's edition.

David M. Hassler, MFA
Managing and Fiction Editor

BEST OF FLYING ISLAND 2014

COLLECTED POETRY

HAPPY ST. PADDY'S DAY

DAN CARPENTER

I remember it best as the best of excuses
for cutting class and getting drunk and kidding yourself
that you looked as good to the girls shedding their winter
pelts
and inhibitions as they looked to you;
that their green tongues said go.

It came to reside, with New Year's Eve,
in that locked upstairs room of the mind and heart
kept by the loved ones of alcoholics;
misshapen mockery of faith, flag and sex,
lost youth leering beneath a green plastic derby.

With you in my March, I open again to the phony
sodden clamor,
extend my thousand Irish welcomes to the daytime
drunks,
the knob-kneed parochial step dancers, the corsaged
politicians,
all the flaunters of the color the singer reminds us
my ancestors wore at the risk of their shabby lives.

With you in my retreat, across the miles, as they say,
I say to them, Yes, you are, all of you, please, be Irish
for one afternoon, herded away downtown, insane and
innocent
of Yeats, of hunger, of my toothless coal-miner
grandparents;
of the pair of us, colorblind, deaf to your drums, free,
green, locked in song.

MANIFEST DESTINY

GEORGE KALAMARAS

Feel free to induce me. Press your breath against my
breath.
Stick your finger down the lorikeet's throat and expel the
sleep medicines.

Ask me for a blanket and I will produce a thread.
We can each hold an end and vibrate a song in praise of
pioneers.

The Conestoga part of my heart can only let you in a
little.
I will gladly feed you beans and lard, watch the flames
pony-prance untamed
    shadows across your face.

We have the same connective tissue inside our more-
than-private bodies.
It resembles a very long river, difficult to cross.

If I were an antelope, you might be a prairie hare.
If I a sheep, you, an Australian cattle dog.

We have known one another throughout many
incarnations.
One time I came to you as lightning, you, the fierce,
almost-soothing rain.

FOR THE NOT YET DEAD

GEORGE KALAMARAS

The other, the one who does not want to die.
I must be absolutely sure of his name
for I do not want to call him
Nikephoros Gregoras or *Georgias*.

His touch throughout the tiles
of the house is that of the newly wed.
And this reverence applies even to dust,
an old coin, a fallen grain
of quinoa that might contain pieces of moon.

We are told that somewhere exists
a pair of better hands. We don't believe
in hands, or even in the word *We*.
We believe in Epsom salts.
A softening from the bath.

A woman is scarved in roses, dealing cards.
The faces are blank, except
the Jack of Pronouns,
the Queen of Blades.
They've finally come to remove the tree
from the ground of this word
or that. I must memorize its name, swirl
of bark, totems in the unwept grain.
Call it quinoa. Call it elm. Call its touch
back into my once lovely untouched mouth.

SMARTY YOU ROUÉ

LESLIE LYNNTON FULLER

Smarty
Stop telling every woman you know
that you love her.

It's like me saying
come get the pussy!
the ex said it tastes like banana!

cupid's handyman, your week
spent on the run
you help women with puppies,
overheating car, malfunctioning toilet

all from the goodness of your heart.
my dear at this age
plumbing is foreplay.

give your ex's son a tennis lesson,
she dreams you're the new stepdad
never mean to hurt anyone.

daddy you're the nightmare on Meridian Street

you do have your ways

when you kiss me,
you massage my
Superior Labial Frenulum
(under the top lip near the gum, I looked it up)
and pretend you're doing oral

please
you can't even kiss without being a tease

oh Smarty you roué
working that boyish charm
into your 90s and in the nursing home
staff will search room by room

see which bed you've landed in.

you'll request a female undertaker
one last chance to vamp
stone dead with a smile on your face
knowing she'll lift the sheet

IT'S NOT THE HEAT, IT'S THE MORTALITY

ANNE HAINES

It was the hottest summer anyone could remember.
I know Texans laugh at twenty, twenty-one days of
ninety
but some afternoons the air was so thick with humidity
you could have spread it on a birthday cake.
Animals died at the county fair, the grand
champion hog smothered in his own incipient bacon,
lambs panting behind the lemon shake-up stand.
Even my sunflowers, bobbing and weaving in the front
yard
like stunned prizefighters, let their leaves wither,
collapse like old women's hands that have given up on
prayer.
Seasons like that, everything feels like a warning.
And when the nights are no relief, the dark air limp and
lowering,
we lie as still as possible in separate beds
listening to the dense hum of crickets,
listening past them to the distant yip of a coyote,
past that to the slow machine of weather
churning in the distance, in the moonlight's steam,
in the unavoidable swelter of August's waking dream.

OUR BREAKUP

JENNIFER HURLEY

The afternoon air smells of summer rain, almost
overpowering the reek of bacon and onion fried
early for the German potato salad that you love.

I cook in the morning so the flavors will
grow more distinct after having time to settle
and melt into each other how we once did.

We once did.

Before disappearing for work you used to leave
notes under your coffee mug, the paper stained
brown from little spills—a watercolor

of a white-spotted deer's hide. I always imagined
a fawn, your handwritten words crossed legs
standing for the first time, clumsy wobbly.

But last night when I tried to care for you,
checked mangy fur for ticks and signs of other
disease, your natural camouflage soon hid you

in a thick part of the forest, a forest I continue
to search, now falling asleep cold alone in a pile
of knotty pine branches and slippery sodden leaves.

COLD PROMISE

JAYNE MAREK

So rare to have the windows open in autumn
  On a day when the dry leaves click together
    Stirred by a robin's foot. Still here, bird?
You'll be sorry if you linger too long
  Among patches of thinning grass.

Beetle buzz, bark scents waft in,
  On damp weedy air. It's morning,
    Time for the lawn to decide: rot or parch?
Irregular patches of light fall
  Timidly from the east, disbelieving

And with good reason. By nightfall, wind
  Will steady its stream across these surfaces,
    The scoured house walls, the shivering glass,
Whistling shingles, all the early promise
  Shoved away by stiff arms.

SCORPIO WRECKING BALL

NORBERT KRAPF

I'm your Scorpio wrecking ball,
the red pepper in your soup,
the flash of pain in your belly.

Oh I can sing it intense,
I got the gut-bucket blues
deep down in my psyche

but I can see the stars
when they flash and sometimes
I climb the ladder higher and higher.

If you're the one listens well
I'll sneak into your office and let
my roiling guts spill in your truth chair.

I bet you'll even smile ever so slow
and sweet and offer me herbal tea.
That's when I go ballistic, baby,

quoting the prophets and visionaries
before you put a hand on my shoulder
and tap me into good-boy submission.

Come on outside and we'll howl together
in harmony at the full moon over our heads
before it's time to head back to the cabin.

You wouldn't believe how calm
I can become when the time is right.
Sit with me, stare into my animal eyes.

A BIRD OF PREY ALWAYS HAS THE LAST WORD

TRACY MISHKIN

FOR SHERRY CHANDLER

I. Letter from Hawk on Christmas Day
Thank you for filling the feeder
and luring the cardinal down.
I was hungry, perched in a pine
and waiting. Fat target. Easy prey.
I suppose you sought beauty: red bird,
evergreens, fresh snow.
I thought only of meat.

II. Reply to Hawk
The Currier & Ives notecard
was a lovely touch. I know
you have to eat. Why rub it in?
Today I bought every can and box
on sale, all for the food bank.
When the season of warmth and giving
is over, donations drop. Like you,
the children have to eat.
They are not sentimental
about their food.

III. Hawk Drops One Last Note
A donation in my honor?
Precious. When I have children
I cannot feed, they shrivel
in the nest and I watch them die.

WINTER NOISE

LYLANNE MUSSELMAN

Listen to the echoes
in the heart of winter: snow
shovels scrape concrete,
tires roll over brittle ice,
arthritic tree branches
pop and crack as they move
in the whistling breeze.

Canada geese
trumpet their flight across
the crisp bright sky, and
like parachutists
smaller feathered friends
drop in at full feeders, chirp
delight while seeds shuffle
onto frozen ground.

One unexpected day,
after months of muffled noise
suffered under too much snowfall,
you will hear the constant dripping
of shiny icicles —
winter's suicidal melt,
drumming in spring sounds.

HOW TO STEAL A PIANO
A PROSE POEM
THOMAS ALAN ORR

Carefully, of course. Keep this in mind: you must not be tempted to play "Heart and Soul" or "Chopsticks" as you lower her through a window on pulleys at two in the morning. Don't let her bang against the side of the building on the way down lest she belly forth with fragments of Chopin or Jelly Roll Morton. Most say the stronger man should stay above, working the ropes, but you need more muscle down below in case a wind comes up and she starts to kick and buck. You don't want to waste time picking up sharps and flats on the street. Tuck her into the bed of the truck and wrap her well. Nobody likes a chilly upright or a cold baby grand. Wool socks on the pedal lyres keep her quiet. And don't drop the fallboard on your fingers or else you'll be singing. Driving through rough streets, avoid the potholes or the whippen will come loose, composing melodies to charm a ghost. A haunted grand, though rare, won't bring a hundred grand.

YOUR SUMMER AT FERNWOOD

JEFFREY OWEN PEARSON

because men were forbidden
in your room
we camped deep in the hardwoods
where two streams slipped
into one

it always rained
and skin stuck to skin
in a glorious sweat

you joked every time I came
the blankets were a tent
and you need bring no poles

at first light when we walked among
the wild bergamot
and prairie blazing stars
hummingbirds suckled
near your breasts

late summer
the rocket grass
fired red
like a beautiful disaster

DRIVING TO THE STARDUST BUFFET

RICHARD PFLUM

I remember the *tick* of the beginning,
now hear the *tock* of the continuing,
and from between the *tock* and the *tick*,
a more rhythmic pounding of the *nothing*.

I have gone out to gather in my sustenance:
some ions, neutral atoms, many neutrons and
protons with a limited number of quarks and
the rare and very small boson. Electrons and
positrons have been combined into rich sauces
and beside them are the colorful and sparkling quanta,
garnished with neutrinos. It is all laid out on
a black presentation board on a counter top:
this stuff I am and need, things some stars
     no longer have any use for.

Still, I feel sometimes that I am a byproduct of
some other more generous nature as I drive into
the parking lot, very crowded now with its
rolling ambience of charged bodies blinking
their lights on and off as a crowd awaits beside
the *event horizon* gate and a doorman, liveried
with the letter "G," presses the button,
     allows all without, inside.

WRESTLING ALLIGATORS

STEPHEN R. ROBERTS

The story of the man who lost an arm
to an alligator in a lake down in Florida
makes me think I should put my arms
around these words in a reptilian intimacy,
hug my pets while they're young
and still small enough to accept such
displays of love or whatever they call it.

I should do this at an early stage of development
because it can be difficult to concentrate
as an arm is being pulled from its socket
in a crocodilian water-dance by a stanza
easily confused with rapture or infatuation.

Mayhem and motive may be misconstrued,
the same as alliteration, if underfed
or overused while ligaments, muscles,
and the mind are being stretched
and torn beyond their capabilities
of elasticity or accommodation.

So I rub the bellies of the little beasts.
Place my pen to paper, deceptively revise
the entranced, undulating bodies to feel
the heat of cold-blooded words unwind.

WINTER DREAM

MARY SEXSON

The winter storm effect brings crowds
to the stores, lines to stand in,
the most coveted items sold out,
and we wait, see if our patience holds.

Late tonight I want to wake up
and make note of the snow,
count the flakes and guess their
accumulations, I want to gaze out

the upstairs window and look down
on the literal abundance of it, enough
to hold us all in, keep us to our chairs
and couches, books opened, movies on,

popcorn popped, the interior
defined by our presence, our gaze
to the fire, we will use words like
cozy and snug, we will chuckle softly
as we get another blanket from the basket.

HEATHCLIFF AND CATHERINE AND ALL THE OTHERS

JO BARBARA TAYLOR

I found an old letter in a library book,
the stamp Brazilian, the missive
in English, a feminine hand
on monogrammed linen stationery,
now yellowed.

August 31, 1922

Dear Carlos—

> *I sit on the terrace—you can picture the emerald*
> *Atlantic*
> *and hear it slapping rocks below—my handkerchief close,*
> *for I will use it, I am sure, before I sign my name below.*
> *On the table, your favorite breakfast item—a chocolat*
> *éclair*
> *and your favorite relic, the rusty lock without its key.*
> *The air is fever. My tears fall already like tropic rain.*
> *I say adieu. Please do not come again maureen. I know you*
> *ask why.*
> *No answer I have is pleasing. I hold your heavy lock in my*
> *hand,*
> *consign it to my heart. I taste you in the delicate éclair,*
> *find you delicious. I glance through our time and smile.*
> *You must know I have loved.*

You, ever in my thoughts—
Amelita

I folded the letter into its envelope,
returned it to *Wuthering Heights,*
thought of all the abandoned lovers,
me included.

THUMBS

HELEN TOWNSEND

I have my father's thumbs.
I first noticed them on a summer
road trip, when no teenager
wants to ride cross country
in a Ford Taurus
with Mom and Dad.
From a bored stare
from the back seat
I first saw the thumbs
on the hands grasping the steering wheel
were the thumbs
on the hands holding my book.

We pray to remember who we are.
That's what Sr. Christina taught
from inside her cavern of black fabric
under reprints of Jesus and Mary.
I didn't know yet
that I carry my icons on me.

BEST OF FLYING ISLAND 2014

COLLECTED FICTION

AMERICAN GRACE
JAMES FIGY

The people of Kemp, Indiana, had all assembled with
their improvised torches—but no pitchforks. Instead
they carried bats and unused rackets from cheap
badminton sets, along with crowbars and oversized
monkey wrenches from the Kemp Spring Factory.

The crowd chanted, "Ho hum, humdrum; Billy Guy has
come."

They packed the crumbling concrete bridge—the only
way out of the north-central Indiana town—suicidally
tight. A reporter from *The Kempee Tribune* took photos
of the whole thing.

It would have been tough for Billy Guy to drive through
the crowd if he'd had a bulldozer. So the chances of his
blue '62 Volkswagen Beetle making it probably did not
exist.

He stopped the car on top of a huge metal plate, the kind
the Kemp Dept. of Minimal Public Works workers used
after they cut into the road. He pushed in the clutch and
pulled the shifter to neutral, then stepped out of the
Volkswagen. His stocky frame towered above the vehicle,
begging the question how he fit in the first place.

"Did the entire town show up to block me in?"

Billy scratched his short goatee while scanning the crowd.

He saw Mrs. Brumer, his ex-girlfriend's mom. She was the reason for all of this, he thought. He would have stayed in Kemp forever, so long as he didn't have to move out of her house.

In her last ultimatum, she had opined that it was awkward for him to live there, as her daughter was getting married in the living room in less than a week. She said she didn't want him running in theatrically from the bathroom to object or following them on their honeymoon to Peru.

"I wish I got to go to Peru," Billy had muttered.

"Bill, I mean Peru, Indiana."

"Oh my god, I know," he had retorted. "It has all the circuses and like the only Taco John's east of the Mississippi."

"Well, you can drive to Taco John's if you live in that apartment above Billings Bail Bonds on Broadway and Main."

When he said he decided to move back to Indianapolis, she had flipped. She said that getting kicked out was no reason to be rude.

"You have to understand by now how this small town works," she said. "I'm not saying you don't have to leave. I'm just saying you can't."

"So it's like the Hotel California? Is it, Mrs. Brumer?"

"Yes and no. You can never leave, but you can't check out anytime you like. You have to do that by this Friday."

The frumpish, forty-something woman faded into the crowd. Everyone blurred together into a solitary mass, hell-bent on keeping the town intact. The crowd did not respond to Billy's question but continued chanting, "Ho hum, humdrum; Billy Guy has come."

He scratched his forehead and shouted, "What is this? The fucking Lord of the Rings? You guys have a song and everything?"

They again chanted, "Ho hum, humdrum; Billy Guy has come," shouting the last word. Then there was complete silence. Well, except for the crackling flames and the uneven idle of the Volkswagen, there was complete silence. And some cicadas were making a terrible racket, but that's not important.

Anyway, a hooded man stepped from the crowd and into the empty street between Billy and the bridge. He pulled the dark hood away to reveal himself as Old Man Todd, the director of conformance at the spring factory.

"Bill," he said, "I brought these people here to put an end to your madness. You can't leave, Bill. Once a Kempee, always a Kempee, and you made that choice."

The day before, Old Man Todd had pulled him aside in the spring factory and warned him. It wasn't safe, he had said, outside Kemp limits.

"George Jefferson said something like: the government that governs the best is the one that controls the least shit. And, I mean, nowadays they want to control pretty much everything about our lives. It ain't right. The government doesn't need to tell anybody where to go, or keep track of everything they do," he had warned. "That's why you have neighbors."

As the crowd began to slowly edge towards him, Billy shook his head. "You're wrong," he said, stroking his goatee. It seemed even more majestic in the torches' glow. He lifted a small remote from his pocket. "As soon as I pull this trigger, something magical will happen that will make you people regret everything."

That statement confirmed what most Kempees had thought all along.

"Terrorist, murderer," they screamed, backing away. "Put your bomb away, terrorist."

But Billy did not have a bomb. It wouldn't have served his purpose. He knew this because he had, in fact, considered using an explosion. But if all his test models were accurate, the glorious explosion would've left Billy melted and relatively unmoved. On Mrs. Brumer's back stoop, twenty little, green army men (turned liquid) had proved this. And *The Kempee Tribune* later noted this detail: "Precisely twenty brave soldiers were sacrificed by and for Billy Guy."

Instead, after hours of overtime and working late into the night when few other people were around, Billy had built and installed a mechanism to ensure escape.

"Calm down, everyone. I'll take care of this," Old Man Todd reassured the crowd. "Only one thing can save us from terrorists—since it's too late for preemptive strikes—and that thing's a prayer." Everyone, except Billy Guy, bowed their heads, and Old Man Todd prayed: "Oh Lord, our Lord, protect us. We know not the things that we have done, nor the things that we have not known that we have not done. Nor have we done the things that we have not known that we might do sometime in the future if thou giveth us the wisdom to figure out how to steal thine neighbor's cable until Judgment Day, which is probably the worst of all sins.

"Give us this day our daily breads, and their liquid counterpart if thou be'est so merciful. And please forgive Billy Guy for trespassing upon us as we have trespassed into his car and stolen cigarettes once or twice—maybe four times. Well, no more than five.

"In thou'st heavenly name and precocious name, Amen," he coughed. And he continued coughing, getting into a regular fit.

As others rushed to help a doubled-over Old Man Todd, Billy stepped back into his bug. He pushed in the clutch and shifted into first gear. With his finger on the trigger, he was ready to make that bug fly like a butterfly—or, maybe, jump like a flea.

Because beneath the metal plate on which he was parked was a gargantuan spring, wound up and ready to throw—no, ready to fire Billy Guy through the midnight air and out of the town of Kemp, Indiana.

"Good riddance to this reverse-picaresque," he shouted. "For forever and always."

Later, when Billy would describe what happened after he pulled the trigger, releasing the spring that sat below the metal plate that sat below his blue Volkswagen bug in which he sat, he would begin like this:

"I never moved. The Earth did.

"My spring jettisoned the planet into the sky, and as it floated down, it rotated just slightly so that the Earth landed on me at the point of Peru, Indiana—on an empty freight car headed out with a circus train. The sun rotated to early afternoon."

A dark, Italian ringmaster made his way back along the tops of cars, holding his top hat in place, to where my bug was situated.

"That was amazing," he said. "Come with me; we just got Taco John's."

He led me to the front of the train, hopping from car to car. His red coattails flapped in the wind. We climbed down into a chic party car with red velvet upholstery, inlaid with golden trim. Two chimps in mauve monkey suits, all bow-tied and cuff-linked, carried over four tall glasses filled with vodka and fresh-squeezed orange juice.

A trapeze artist—from Canada of all places—asked, "How did you pull off said feat and still maintain such American grace, eh?"

"Who is Charlie?" he asks again, this time an actual, existential question.

He raises his face again to catch his reflection in the strip of mirror. Hold. Don't look away.

13 Across. Five letter word for Without Another.

He throws down the pen. It rolls to the middle of the newspaper, rocking in the crease between the pages. He picks up the remainder of a fish taco in his right hand, but his fingers tremble and he drops it back on the plate. The thing falls open and the lettuce flops wetly across the table and onto the floor.

"You'll never use your left hand again," the doctor had told him. "Fortunately, your right hand will be relatively functional with some physical therapy. You are right-handed?"

"No," Charlie said, keeping his voice low. As if not saying it out loud would make it less true.

"Well," the doctor said, leaving it at that.

That was when people were still shooting him sympathetic smiles. Bandages still covered his face. The extent of the damage wasn't obvious at a glance. There was still hope.

"Are you ready for your check, sir?"

The waitress stands at his elbow, just outside his field of vision. He turns and looks her right in the eye, just to see her quail.

"More coffee, please," he says, even though he doesn't want any more. *I'm cruel*, he thinks. She practically runs to the hot plate, but she's taking her time coming back. When she does return, she drops the check facedown beside his cup.

The shell-pink over the Gulf is fading to gray beyond Sunset Key when he steps outside. He has the rolled up back page of the newspaper in his right hand. Maybe he'll finish the crossword. Or maybe he'll fold it into a paper boat and drop it off the pier.

Of course he won't do that. You can't fold a paper boat with one hand.

He stuffs it into his back pocket. The long, pale roll sticks straight up and catches in his shirt. He walks slowly even though he doesn't have to. It's a miracle, the doctor said, that your legs weren't affected.

Miracle. People throw that word around. It's a miracle you're alive, Charlie. That you get to live the next fifty years as a shell of your former self. 13 Across. ALONE.

When he reaches the path that meanders toward the pier along the highest dune of the beach, the sun has dropped to the edge of the horizon, floating behind an orangey film, dulling its light, the Gulf swallowing its reflection. There are still plenty of people on the sand—tangled legs on beach blankets, sandy hair, and string bikinis. Key

West, the land of lovers. As they're heading back from the beach, swarming like ants over the grassy dunes, he's going against the traffic, cleaving a path through them on his way to the pier. Its sea-bleached rails rise ghostlike over the waving grasses. He's almost there.

He pushes off the sand with each step. Push a little harder, and maybe you'll take off. The earth will release you and you'll be gone.

On the twilit shore, he becomes a shadowy figure. Nameless and faceless, but he likes it that way. He isn't a monster anymore, just a silhouette on the beach. A salty breeze sweeps in off the Gulf and there's a note in it that catches in his good ear. An acoustic sound that reminds him of a song he used to like. His eye twitches involuntarily. The one he can see with. A grain of sand, or perhaps the angle of the wind.

A mist is forming on the surface of the water, rolling onto the shore. A single street lamp sends a white spotlight onto the pier. He aims for it. He'll cross the circle of light and plunge again into that dim obscurity: a cloud of mist over a dark sea where no one will see him. The lure of darkness is stronger now that he has tasted it. The wood makes a soggy *clunk clunk* beneath his feet as he walks, quicker now. The rhythm of his steps soothes him with its normalcy.

A couple, kissing under the light, separate when they see him. His hunched posture, his averted gaze. Their receding footsteps as they head back to the beach. A peal of female laughter. He passed with them to his right, so they hadn't seen the disfigured portion of his face. If they had, they might be frightened rather than amused.

Her laugh sounds familiar, if foreign. Her laughter. Emily's. She was always laughing, even at the end.

Outside the circle of light, he leans heavily on the railing, staring down into the swirling sea. A bit of foam bobs on the surface, pulling apart, riding the slopping water, and washing up on the sand.

"I know who you are." A voice from off to his right.

"It's a small town. Everyone knows who I am," he says without turning. It's always startling to him when he speaks out loud and the unfamiliar ring of his voice meets his good ear. *Everyone knows me except for me.*

"Charlie Throne," the woman says. "I read about you."

He leans farther over the railing. It's his habit to turn his face away. He isn't used to being addressed on purpose and doesn't know how to respond. She lapses into silence but he can feel her presence beside him still. He turns quickly and looks right at her. She'll see his face. She'll leave him alone.

She's leaning forward, forearms on the railing, chin on her arms. She looks back at him steadily. He watches her eyes, the corners of her mouth, waiting for a reaction, but there isn't one. She looks bored. He breaks eye contact first. He hasn't been the first one to break eye contact with anyone in two years. He keeps track. Lately, there's no eye contact at all. Even the doctors, though he's pretty much done seeing them now.

There may be something a surgeon can do, a friend had said. His eyes trained on Charlie's chest, his hair, out the window, anywhere but on his face. "For a cosmetic surgeon I know," he said, slipping a business card into Charlie's hand. The good hand, of course, though he didn't touch it more than necessary.

"Can he raise the dead?" Charlie had asked. He hasn't seen that friend in a long time.

It was strange at first, that awkward looking away, but it's expected now. It's the prolonged eye contact that's the strange thing. When he looked at himself in a mirror, he couldn't understand how anyone looked at him at all.

"It's not easy, is it? Living like this." She had been staring at the disfigured mask of his face, but she isn't looking now. Her arms are dangling over the edge as if she's reaching for the sea. He glances at her left hand. No ring, but the indentation where possibly one once sat.

"I don't want your pity," he says coldly. It comes so quickly to his lips it's like it had been forming in the back of his throat since the beginning and he finally let it out. He breathes out. A sound like relief.

"Why not?" she asks. Her voice is the coo of a dove. "I would."

He looks at her sideways. She's younger than she sounds, maybe his own age, with blonde hair curling around her shoulders. It shifts in the salt air and veils the side of her face. She has that sad expression that many women wear in the gray region between their late twenties and their mid-thirties. The period where they haven't yet reconciled to growing into women and haven't yet given up being girls. Emily had that look.

He presses his chest to the railing to feel the pressure on his lungs.

The cool air reminds him of that night. He and Emily had met for dinner downtown, right near the taco place where he was tonight. They had both worked in the Historic Seaport area of town, but this one time they had driven separate cars because Emily had been running late in the morning. Funny how a little impatience and a decision like that—Charlie deciding he couldn't wait for her that morning—becomes a turning point. When he thought back to that day he barely remembered how important he had thought that meeting with his newest client was for his career, he only relived the way he grabbed his laptop and tossed her keys on the counter. "Sorry, babe, I've got to go without you. I'll meet you after work." They had planned to come to the pier for a moonlight walk after dinner but at the last minute Emily changed her mind, said she wanted to get home. No reason given, and he never knew what it was. He followed her, listening to an acoustic album he loved. Bon Iver. A sad album all about heartbreak he felt drawn to, but couldn't fully grasp. Not then.

He never could remember exactly why he hadn't seen it happen. He must have zoned out, let his mind drift into the wordless obscurity of the music, dropping farther and farther behind her. When her car streaked suddenly across the two lanes of the Overseas Highway, it took him a second to register that it was her. He swore his heart stopped as he watched helplessly: her car rolling down the embankment and righting itself as it landed, rocking in the crease between the road and the narrow strip of land. The water's edge only a few feet away. It happened like a dream. Slow motion. Silent. Its cause unclear.

The woman on the pier reaches over and rests her hand on his. He stares at it. The soft, white skin of her hand on the mottled flesh of his own. She wraps her fingers around his. Two years, he thinks.

He slammed on the brakes and skidded onto the shoulder of the highway. Ran down the embankment, tripping and sliding on the sand and gravel. Wasted how many seconds rushing to the driver's side to find it crushed shut. He wrenched open the passenger door and she was there, her limp body leaning over the console. Her eyes filled with terror like a trapped animal. Stuck in her seatbelt.

She reached for his hand. It was the last time someone held his hand for the sake of holding his hand.

"It's going to be okay," the woman next to him says. Pulling him out of his memory.

"It's not going to be okay," he says, wrenching his hand back. He's instantly sorry. "You're trying to make it seem like it isn't that bad," he says.

"No. I'm not," she says. The thrumming of the waves counted out three beats. "It *is* that bad, isn't it?"

"It's worse," he says.

"Exactly."

He waits ten seconds. Thirty seconds.

Doctors telling him everything was going to be fine, even though nothing was going to be fine. Family members pretending to pat him on the back but not touching him, telling him he should move on with his life. Emily would've wanted that. But Charlie wonders whether Emily would've wanted him if she was still around. Who would? He wouldn't have blamed her.

He isn't used to someone giving him the truth. Treating him like a fellow human being. Then again, she's standing to his right, the side that hadn't taken the brunt of the fire. From there she could see a perfectly normal ear, the smooth skin of his neck, and if she focused on that, she would barely even notice the melted flesh on his cheek and the reconstruction of his nose, nostrils reformed so he can breathe. Whatever pleasure he feels in the moment, he doesn't feel like delaying the inevitable. So he turns, facing her head on.

"Look at me," he says. "Really look. I dare you."

Her arms are lying again on the top rail of the pier, and her body hunched over. She looks up. Raises an eyebrow. "What's wrong?" she asks. No grimace, no turning away.

"Look at me."

"I am."

"Doesn't it make you sick to look at me?"

She stands up straight, looking him right in the eye.

"Does it make you sick looking at me?" she asks.

"Of course not," he says.

"Well," she says. Leaving it at that.

"What?"

A tear is running down her cheek now.

"May I hug you?" She says it softly like she's afraid to ask for such a great favor.

They are staring into each other's faces and he swallows. His mouth is dry. It's a side effect, and this time something else.

"I . . . " he says, but something catches in his throat and he can't finish. She doesn't wait for an answer. Wraps her arms around his waist and rests her cheek on his chest. Something swells there in his breast. Something he hasn't felt for a long time. It all comes flooding back. The feelings. The memories.

He had climbed into the passenger seat and grabbed the buckle of her seat belt. The smell of gasoline burned the back of his throat. Pulled on the buckle with his left hand. It wouldn't give. The left side of his body faced her. She whispered, "Charlie," and he turned partway toward her, her name on his lips. She laughed. A what-the-hell-have-I-done laugh. And then a flash of blinding light. He had tried to call to her.

That was it. That was the memory. He had awakened from the coma three weeks later and finished shouting her name through the slit cut into the bandage for his mouth.

A tear tugs at the corner of his right eye. He can't cry much, but the tears pinch his eyelids and threaten to form. Sometimes he wishes they would. The woman is still holding him, cradling him against her even though his own arms are at his side. Slowly he raises his right arm and runs his hand over her shoulder. She begins to sob. Great heaving sobs into his shirt.

"I understand," he says. "My face makes me sad too."

She only cries harder.

"I'm not crying because you're ugly," she chokes. "I'm crying because you're beautiful." She presses her palm against his chest. "Here. And you've forgotten it."

Charlie laughs. Then he stops, startled by the sound of it coming from his own mouth. His voice sounds different, but his laugh the same. It feels the same, the way it vibrates through his chest and tickles the inside of his mouth. It feels good to laugh. Like coming home.

"I'm sorry," she says, stepping back. "I didn't mean . . . "

"It's okay," he says.

He smiles, but follows it quickly with a frown. He's seen the effect a smile has on his face. It's not a real smile. It's a gaping wound.

"It's nice," he says, but he doesn't finish. Being touched, he means. Kindness.

"It's hard sometimes," she whispers. "Being alone. I saw you and I thought you might understand."

She isn't looking now. She's staring at a spot between their feet, so he stares at it, too.

"I don't think it ever stops hurting," he says. It's not the right thing to say maybe, but it's what he thinks. It's the truth.

"That's heartbreak, Charlie," she says. "You walk away scarred. Everyone does. You just got the worst of it. You wear your heartbreak on the outside, too."

He stands still. Waiting. This is a turning point. At the restaurant, he didn't know, but when he reached the pier he had crossed a threshold into another lifetime. Like when he'd jumped from his car on the side of the highway. The last moments of one life before the start of another one. Another consciousness.

"Wait," he says. But she hasn't moved. She looks up.

"You miss her," she whispers, touching her fingertips just under his chin. He flinches at the unexpected touch, but doesn't pull away. "But you miss you, too," she adds. "And that's okay."

She reaches into his back pocket and pulls out the newspaper. Scribbles something on the corner of the sheet, and in the center of the crossword. She presses it into his hand.

"Will you do me a favor?" she asks. "Please."

"Anything," he says. He realizes that might be true.

"Remember this," she says. "Everyone is sadder than you think they are."

He searches her eyes. Searching for the subtext.

"You're not alone," she whispers. Stretching onto her toes. She presses her lips gently to his cheek. A place where he has enough feeling to recognize the action. "You're not alone," she says again.

"Who are you?" he whispers.

"Call me," she says. "Please."

She's written her phone number on the edge of the newspaper, and her name, Olive, printed in five squares of the crossword. Meeting Charlie's name at the "I." He brushes his finger over the square. Carefully, he folds the paper and returns it to the safety of his pocket. He gazes over the darkening beach, watching as her figure fades into the night.

SPHINX THE HUNTER,
A TALE OF DISCOVERY
ROBIN LOVELACE

I have a black cat named Sphinx. Actually, she is Antoine's cat. But Sphinx still lives here, Antoine does not. A three year marriage and I loved Antoine, truly loved him, but he didn't believe me. He said I couldn't really love him or anybody else for that matter.

I met Antoine when I needed a lawyer to defend me from a hit and run charge. Yes, I was guilty. Yes, I hit someone and left the scene. Only because I was late for work and I didn't need an arrest on my record and I sure didn't need the insurance problems. Later on, we discovered the guy I hit was drunk. He was riding a moped. Swerved out in the street before I could push on the brakes, and I had no previous record. The drunken moped driver lived but had to be in a wheelchair. Actually, it worked out pretty good for him. He didn't die and he was eligible for disability checks so he could sit in his little house and drink up the rest of his little life. I got six months' suspension and had to pay a thousand dollar fine.

Last spring, Antoine met someone else. A fat girl who was three years older than him, with frizzy, brown hair. He didn't tell me about her, ever. No, he said he was working out at the gym when he was gone so much. I found a restaurant receipt in his jacket pocket. After that, I followed him. I never mentioned it, never confronted Antoine, never brought it up to anyone.

Antoine wants to go to Miami. He didn't tell me that either, but I saw on his laptop the history of all the things he was looking up. Apartments for rent in Miami popped up a half dozen times. He said I could have the house that was almost paid off and all the furnishings. He was starting a new life, without me, and if I didn't bother him again and just let him go, I could have the house and everything in it.

He told me he figured me out. That he thought I was a sociopath and on a couple occasions, he saw me drop my guard and that my eyes looked dead, like I had no soul and that he was stupid for not seeing that a long time ago. He brought up the time I was really angry at his mother for trying to stop us from getting married, and she was hospitalized because of food poisoning soon after.

Ahhh, but he didn't know about the time my assistant manager called me a name under her breath, and the next week, she had four flat tires in the parking lot, after the mall closed. In the dark. And her cell phone was mysteriously missing from her purse.

Of course I never let him know about the time I broke into my old boyfriend's apartment and unplugged his fridge when he was gone for ten days on his Hawaiian honeymoon (I thought that was rather creative). Wow. Maybe Antoine is right. That all sounds really mean.

Antoine never said his new life was with a fat, frizzy haired, almost middle-aged bitch. Why do some guys go for the fat bitches? I don't understand it. I have a trim body, no jelly rolls, run every morning, and my hair is definitely not frizzy. Anyway, it's over between us. I have the house and the five acres of land and all the beautiful furnishings and a black cat that I don't like very much.

I know of no other black man who owned a cat, but Antoine is an unusual black man, in some ways. He likes rock more than he likes blues or rap. And he is a big fan of Saul Bellow, some Jewish writer I think is dead now. And he likes golf and living in a house that sits on a secluded plot of land with a large swatch of dense woods behind it, snug between the suburbs and the rural cornfields of Indiana. I wonder if he likes Miami now.

I do like dogs. Dogs are sweet, and dogs adore their masters. Dogs are useful for something. Not cats. Sphinx hardly acknowledges me unless she's hungry. She is a good hunter, though, and graceful. Like a ballet dancer. Walking in that light-footed, elegant way. She has a habit of walking toward me, moving semi-speedily, paws positioned just so. When I turn to watch her, she stops. She meows at me. She walks under my desk and pops her head out to look at me. Yellow eyes surrounded by inky black fur. Why the hell does she do that?

Sphinx rarely goes outside but when she does, she always comes back with an animal in her mouth. She has brought back a sparrow, a mourning dove, a baby rabbit, and one time she brought nothing back, but a couple hours later she vomited up three half-digested baby mice. I almost lost my cookies when I saw that mess and cleaning it up was the second most disgusting thing I ever had to do.

After that incident, I have decided to not let her out ever. She would have to be an indoor cat from now on. Doomed to only hunt down those sporadic, annoying crickets that find their way into Antoine's, I mean *my*, beautiful house. Sphinx will have to stay inside, eating only dry cat food and the occasional can of sardines. Fur balls were all I planned to clean up, and hopefully those would be few and far between.

This evening, I opened the door to go out on the back deck and when I swung open the screen door, Sphinx ran out before I could stop her. She streaked down the deck steps and across the back yard and into the woods that grew not twenty yards from Antoine's, excuse me, *my*, back door.

Damn. Hard telling what she was running after and what she would bring back to me.

While I waited for her return, I swept some fallen leaves off of the deck and killed a fat, brown, evil-looking spider with a little black and white triangle on its stomach that spun a web between a bough of the pink rose bush I had planted just a year before and the edge of a deck railing. I have a device that looks like a small tennis racket but when you press and hold in two red buttons on the handle simultaneously, the wires turn electrified and spark burns any bug it touches. I bought it at the hardware store a few years ago, when I knew I'd be living next to a swatch of bug-filled trees and damp undergrowth. It took half a minute to shock the spider to death on the wires of my deadly tennis racket, but I am a patient person. When its spindly legs stopped twitching, I carried it to the toilet, dropped it in, and flushed it.

After I sent the spider to the sewer, I researched big, brown spiders with black and white markings on their stomachs. The Internet told me it was an orb spider. Not poisonous. I had killed an innocent spider. Still, Sphinx had not returned.

I went back in the house but left the door open. Just the screen door was shut and Sphinx had torn a hole through the bottom of the screen to get in last spring, when Antoine was sleeping late one morning (Antoine is a very successful lawyer and he worked long hours during the week) and I was at work. We replaced the screen, and she eventually scratched a hole in the new screen, too. After that, I decided that if Sphinx wanted out that bad, I wouldn't replace the screen again. So I left the torn screen with the hole. She could let herself back in the house.

My favorite crime show was on. I learned a lot from watching it, and the main character was my kind of tough guy. Tonight was the second-to-last episode. I did not want to be disturbed by having to get up and let a meowing cat back into the house, so I left the door open and the screen door locked. A thought about raccoons walking through the hole in the screen flashed through my mind for a moment, but the TV started playing the opening theme music. I had my cup of tea getting cold on the coffee table and my blueberry scone sitting on a plate right next to it. Anyway, the chance of an actual raccoon walking in was little to none. I watched the show. It was my addiction, and I needed my weekly dose.

After the show was over and I was waiting for the previews, Sphinx came padding through the hole in the screen door and into the living room. She had something muddy in her mouth. She dropped it on the beige carpet in front of me as I sat, legs tucked under, on Antoine's (now mine) eggshell-colored suede leather sofa. I scooted closer and took a good look at what awful thing Sphinx had brought to me. It was a piece of something fleshy and sticky wet. It stank.

Crap, I thought, what else was out there stinking up the woods? If a cat could find it, so could one of those damn, drooling bloodhounds. I wanted to kick Sphinx, but I didn't. Actually, I was thankful she brought it to me. I flushed it.

INDIANAVILLE

RANDY WIREMAN

Mint and sweat discolored his t-shirt. He spoke in
fractured sentences, somehow conciliatory, into his cell.
The mint made sense, as there were miles of the stuff just
northwest of the broiler. I remember mint always
hanging in the air near harvest, and this young man must
have been wallowing in that oil all morning, all
afternoon. This town had always been a hub for potatoes,
not necessarily mint. I'd grown up near here in the
Eighties and this broiler had changed names a half dozen
times. Steamy day.

The young man slipped his cell into his pocket as he
waited in line. He scanned the room as he tucked in his
shirt and then wiped his black hair back. He stretched,
taking little notice of me as I stood behind him, much
less what I would think of his green-splotched elbows
and forearms below the carefully rolled denim
shirtsleeves. Glanced toward a man sitting at a table
pushed into the wall near the bathroom and who caught
his eye pretty much deliberately, gave a single nod. His
friend was similar in age and stature. His massive arms
were reddened by long stress marks as if a rope had been
tied around them, though Mint & Sweat's were deeply
tanned and glossy.

Mint & Sweat ordered two BBQs with two large fries
and two large root beers, making sure the round, gray-
haired woman behind the counter heard "large" root
beers correctly. The broiler was still as small as it ever had
been, and the only tables not being used were littered

with the wrappers and cups of the previous customers, customers who must have been quick to eat, to leave, and to never return. Even I was to never come back, or so I thought. This poor town has gotten even poorer. What brought me here had been a stop for gas, tenderloin, and a large reconstituted iced tea before I moved on to Knox for a funeral. My turn for the welcome to Jan's and the tired grin. Damn, out of tenderloin, so sorry.

Indianaville just seemed to have stumbled into existence along Highway 421, where wild roses, swamp grass, and red-shouldered black birds patrolled a staggered margin between agriculture and civilization. Money was always raised on the one side and poured into the other; until, that is, when the green was tapped to other places, to other hands. Set back from the streets, many of the turned-milk clapboard houses were as dreary as they were back when I lived here: cavernous porches ornamented with plastic red carnations or burnt ferns bending over their concrete pots; front yard sand pits peppered with crabgrass and dandelion—seas of sand, crabgrass, and dandelion. Every other house or so had signs propped against tobacco-stained windows warning of dogs or Honeywell Security. Even a couple of Victorians facing the road had become permanent markets for antiques and car parts, displayed on plywood held up by shop horses and rusty metal tables with bent legs. But there was no one in attendance, no one minding the shop in this heat save a black and white cat that lazily crossed the road as I nearly put the steering wheel into my lungs. The cat was as old and stiff as the Fifties street lamps along Main, lit prematurely in the early evening sun. Ghosts stuck in molasses, this town.

I sat at a table in the back, swiped off the spilled salt with a napkin. The next table over sat Mint & Sweat and his friend. I glanced over. They responded with a slight nod. Suspecting they wanted some privacy, I sat facing away from them as much as I could, grabbed some fries from the paper boat, dipped them in some ketchup smelted by the window radiation, and appreciated the salt and grease and vinegary emulsion on my tongue. Could swear I tasted tenderloin and catfish, too. Small towns always taste the same.

Nothing had changed. Same tables, same plywood bathroom door, and same off-white blinds, too, as when I was a teenager. I must have sat in this corner over a hundred times. Out the window I see the edge of Burke's woods where my buddy and I caught anything that moved in the drain creeks. It's all fenced in now. A rich farmer probably bought it. There was Burke's farm at the edge of their woods, and then Ogden's farm where my buddy ended up renting a trailer, and then Mom and Dad's farm, way out near the county line. Indianaville was our closest town; roadside homes, two gas stations, and one broiler where hell-raisers like my buddy and me roamed in outdated Monte Carlos and salmon-colored, convertible Mercs, and a fairly new metallic blue Cutlass we stole from his sister once and steered it right into a drag race on 3rd Street.

"Naw. It's not like that, kid. Crazy. Listen to yourself."

That was Mint & Sweat, in his conciliatory voice. Wondered what they do in this town to pass the time. It was a weekend playground for us before we got our cars. I was happy here for a few summers until we discovered that other worlds were only a gas tank away. 421 broke open, hemorrhaged, and nothing could stop the bleed from Main Street to the steel mills up in Gary or to places south. I guess we just got up and went.

"Less than an hour's difference, Perry. Maybe forty?" Mint & Sweat's friend had a much higher pitch than what his brawn suggested. "We could stay at Regina's place here in town."

"Naw. Jenny's pretty smart." I heard one of them sip their root beer, squeal the straw up and then down. "She's probably heading to Bloomington."

Didn't surprise me none, Jenny leaving Indianaville. Nothing changes here. We were no different. Guess we left everything to the elderly and to the migrant workers to sort out.

"Bloomington?"

Only a few true farmers around here anymore. Poor farmers sold their land to rich farmers and then the rich farmers sold their precious muck to conglomerates. We were poor farmers. Dad sold out to Leon Bailey one acre at a time, more or less. We always had more sand dunes than muck, anyway. Progress, I suppose.

"Yeah. Business school."

I knew the guys were looking around making sure I wasn't listening. Their pauses were too perfectly placed. Their words were heavier than they wanted them to sound. I scooted my chair farther into the table, focused on my fries, and realized a few minutes had passed when neither guy had said anything. The heartbreaking stillness of this town. Really. A car or truck couldn't break it for very long. And the winters, man. Dead. For a teenager, it was frustrating.

"Oberlander's sister lives in Knox."

Too cold to hunt. Depressing, really. Must have burned a million gallons driving from one friend's house to another.

"Debbie's cool about things. Her cousin—"

"Fucking listen to yourself. Why would you work here and live there? Think about it."
Stillness. Then a movement—a rustling—that broke Indianaville, one that struck a nerve. I felt the deep loathing of reality, a wakening from a satisfying fantasy. I hated how the metal chairs squeaked, how the tables wobbled on the cracked and gouged linoleum, banged against the dry, warped window sills.

"JJ."

I stared at the greasy fingerprints on the blue curtains, felt a sudden loneliness in a forever kind of way.

"Just sit your ass down."

And I was familiar with that kind of forever. I know what happens when people leave: they leave others behind.

I smelled underarm deodorant as Mint & Sweat's friend walked past me towards the door where he slammed his food into the wastebasket. His friend yanked on the door, hesitated, held it open for a young, blonde girl and an older woman with matching hair. He glanced back at Mint & Sweat as the women entered. A slight shake of the head? His friend walked out, let the door creak shut behind him.

The girl saw Mint & Sweat in the corner, waved, and then got in line to order their usual. Not sure what Mint & Sweat did. He might have nodded. Didn't matter. There could be no love there, or at least not as much as with the one who walked out. It was obvious. I felt the change in sympathy, in tenderness, in honesty. Mint & Sweat felt it, too. I felt his sense of letting something go, of leaving something behind, leaving something unfinished. A kind of death. He wanted to run out, wanted to make things right. He stayed, in his corner, long enough to hate this moment, this place, the stench of fried food, the ugly old linoleum, the off-color blinds, the stillness.

I finished all I could of the hamburger, a poor second when one longed for tenderloin, longed to get back onto 421. No reason to stay any longer, anyway. Jan's Broiler held a gripping guilt. Mint & Sweat was staring out the window, handsome, massive, tanned at forearm and neck, and ready on a hair-trigger moment to run out the door and find his buddy, leave this altogether. This town was like fingernail impressions in a waxed paper cup, conjuring the strength to escape a lifelong repression, to expose the lie. Or seek safety in it? Wax shavings everywhere.

The lie? Did Mint & Sweat have a sudden hatred of his Baptist lessons, the lessons that he rarely had questioned? When a man really wants something, he goes and gets it. What of their intimacy? Could he hate his girlfriend, too, though by no fault of her own? Hated her mother, those disapproving eyes that could guilt the one-winged Satan. The two were beautifully dressed in matching summer colors, clueless to the complexity that layered a man's heart. Mint & Sweat nodded to his girl, and then he stared into the table at ambiguous initials etched together inside a heart. Might he have carved his buddy's name in the faux marble, between "Class of '77" and "Darlene Loves T.A.L."? But someone in this small town would have recognized his hand, seen him do it.

He should. He should do it, even if Jenny Cole saw him do it. He wrote it out with his green-stained finger, wrote it big using the condensation pooled around his cup. He dared not wipe it away, hoping that someone, anyone, would see it, yes, finally see it! He'd knock down the first one who said anything derogatory, anyone who made a face or dishonored it in any way. He'd leave it there, too. His girl called out his name. He stared into the initials, smelled her perfume. His girl bent down, shook his arm.

"Mamma has a table by the door. Are you all right?"

He dropped a napkin over the wetness, watched his buddy's initials soak through the paper and fade into themselves like gray clouds. She watched him do it. She said nothing and must have thought he was losing it. She'd always be left wondering, perhaps knowing. Jenny's a smart girl.

Suppose I knew what he was going to do next. Mint &
Sweat was going to leave Indianaville. He'd go to the
steel mills up north for a couple of years, and then he'd
go follow his girl to Bloomington, not be passing by here
for another ten years, on his way to Knox for a funeral.
He'd pass Jan's Broiler three blocks north of Main Street,
drive by Burke's woods and past Ogden's little farm
where he'd keep his engine running a field away and
count how many trailers still looked lived in. And then
he'd get back on 421 and drive on through the acres of
mint to the northwest. The fields near Knox would crest
and fall in the restless broil of summer as the mint, ever-
present, would never leave the tongue tasting anything
else.

BEST OF FLYING ISLAND 2014

COLLECTED CREATIVE NONFICTION

THE LITERARY LIFE AND A LITTLE DEATH

DAN CARPENTER

I am fresh from an online debate with bookish friends about one of America's most celebrated living poets when death comes to a family member who shares the poet's name by sheer coincidence and shares a trademark quality of her favorite subject matter: non-humanity.

No sooner do I vent my weariness with Mary Oliver's incessant animal poems than Oliver dies on me; and I must try, against all hope of achieving poetry, to write him a decent eulogy. He earned it: he gave a pet's perfection in his six willful and sporadically violent years, and he may have lasted his full feline half score and five had it not been for my lassitude, my complacency, my wishful thinking that his profound lethargy and pitiable crying of the last day was just one more occasion for a tough little guy to barf out his troubles and trot on. Probably poisoned by some plant or refuse he ingested, the vet surmised. Who knows? Who springs for a $100 autopsy for a cat, especially if it might yield an indictment that he could have been saved?

He died all alone against a chain link fence on a sublime Sunday afternoon, abandoned by the man who fed him, held doors open for him, provided feet around which he curled and gave ounces, if not pints, of blood to his playfulness of tooth and claw. My grief is commensurate with his innocence. My anger and anguish and remorse befit the death of a child. I've never questioned the instructive beauty of Mary's dogs and bears, only their redundancy. She numbed me to the pain of the single speck of the wealth of fauna, lost and lodged in the eyelid and the heart.

Ollie was a ghetto boy, gray even to his whiskers, rescued from a cardboard box of newborns outside an abandoned house by my son. His namesake is a fellow orphan, Oliver Twist. My small comfort: Ollie's life may have ended in days had it not been for Pat's intervention, the whim that brought him to our house, the place whereto all complications converge. He grew from puffball to lean loping miniature panther in that domain, somehow keeping his infant voice, that comic and ultimately pathetic squeak that I heard over and over on his final day and will hear for the length of memory. A cry for help, missed by a lifelong journalist who prides himself on the rare skill of listening.

Such a mousy voice and, sometimes, such a mean little bastard. Those bug eyes would dilate to full round black and he would leap and rip flesh. The lady of the house— also a Mary—would scream for me to seize him and toss him outdoors. And yet... yet there's a feline sensitivity to the environment and its human component that compelled him, when she was convalescing in lonely despondency from a stroke, to post himself at her side and on her lap for hours at a stretch. We choose to believe, anyway, that such were the workings inside his tiny skull.

I labored to exhaustion digging a grave behind the garage, in an overgrown border patch where Oliver was wont to hang out on his pretend-predator forays. The ground was stubborn, ribbed with tree roots, yielding up a brick, a bottle cap, a scrap of black garbage bag. I remember a funeral back here three decades ago when a toddler joined me in saying goodbye to a goldfish named Simon. A tender, made-for-vignette moment, which I duly conveyed in my newspaper column. A light life given for lightweight literature.

Now, the stiff, staring corpse of a family member we all mourn goes into the hole with hard effort, and he and I and my wife make this passage alone. I pull the rocky dirt and dry leaves over my final view of my beloved Ollie, half-wrapped in a ludicrous iridescent green grocery bag, and I slap a broken piece of concrete steppingstone atop lest I forget where the earth reclaimed him, and I kiss my fingers and touch the filthy surface, grateful for the milky sky that will wash his rough bed a few hours hence, trying to be grateful the world has greater miseries than this one that tears at me right now.

SEASONS: FEBRUARY

MAUREEN O'HERN

It was far colder than I expected it to be. I walked quickly into the breeze that carried the whooshing of the water from the nearby creek. I pulled my cocoon of sweatshirts closer and wondered which was more chilling, the late-winter breeze or the sound of the winter water. As I followed the creek, its gurgling *sotto voce* mimicked my rapid pace.

I had walked there many times, listening intently to the creek's susurrate mystical language, unintelligible to me yet tantalizingly word-like. It was always trying to tell me something that I couldn't understand.

The trees along the banks were brown and bare, crowded as though seeking warmth from each other, lifting as supplicant bony fingers to the featureless white sky. Except for one, which mutely called to me. I stopped, puzzling. Then slowly, over spongy early-spring ground, with a mysterious sense of presence, I approached it. The creek ran smooth there, silky and subdued.

That tree was darker than the others, and it wasn't just beseeching; it was screaming. Long thorns burst from its branches and a spiral of thorns entwined it. How had I not seen its pain before, and why did it seem familiar to me? It was at once new and known. Why? What was it? The winter-bound trees stretching their scraggly fingers to the pallid sky, the black tree with its girdle of thorns— they settled in me and unsettled me. What was it?

I continued on my walk, chilled in a different way, slowed, turning again and again to look back at that tree as it gradually receded into the wooded tangle, assuming its previous anonymity. *What was it?*

Days later it came: Dachau. The memorial sculpture. The same frozen reaching, the same silent screams, the same motionless writhing. In the background the ovens I would not walk through. I had had no thought of encountering such a thing on my walk. I wasn't looking for it. But there it was and will be, every leafless February.

How is it that some things in our daily landscapes are suddenly seen with a new eye? How is it that something so obvious—like pain—can be hidden? Were these the mysteries carried in the current of the creek?

The Dachau agonies and the cold trees grasped at the same indifferent sky. Is it by accident or design that I saw the one in the other? No matter. Enough that I did.

CHANGE

TERI COSTELLO

It was winter. I wore the uniform, suits and high heels, hairdos and makeup. My charcoal wool suit had a slit up the back of the skirt, just enough.

Meeting each week to strategize with the boys at the downtown office, I made recommendations to improve their accounting. They were my age—early forties. Young Turks. The conversations were smart. I was hitting my professional stride. I knew what I was about, what they were about, what they needed, and how to deliver. Good times.

In a singular moment, walking down the hall to one of those meetings (it was a Wednesday), my world changed forever. I felt the earth move under my feet, like the song said—but not in a good way. As I entered the conference room, all heads turned, all eyes were on me, mesmerized by the worms slithering out of my nose, mouth, and ears, the flames shooting out of the top of my head.

I started to speak and couldn't put two thoughts together. Most of my vocabulary was gone, and I could manage only short, awkward squeaks—this as sweat rolled down my back, legs, neck, and face. I looked down, trying to compose myself, and the glassy eyes of my coldcocked self-esteem stared up at me from the carpet. I thought I was dying.

"Is it warm in here?"

"No."

Sparklers began to fly across my mind's eye. Maybe they were *in* my eyes. Maybe I was having a stroke. Maybe there *were* no little sparklers.

After two weeks, I called the doctor. I told him I had lost the ability to comprehend simple concepts, my communication skills were gone, and I had gained sparklers, worms, sweat, and oh, a logic-blinding, generalized fury.

He told me to come in and give a blood sample, that he would see me when the results were back. And he'd put a rush on that. He said, "I am going to leave the phone now, sweetie, but Natalie will come on the line, and she will set these appointments up for you. Okay?"

"Okay," I whispered.

Thank God—the man knew I was losing my grip and had just attached a lifeline from him to me. Or, he was just trying to get rid of me—the old Natalie trick. He probably used it every time crazy people called him.

A week later I sat in his office.

"You're too young for this to be happening now," he said, "but it is. Your hormone activity has completely shut down."

I laid my head on his shoulder and cried for forty-five minutes—he's that kind of doctor. I finally gave him a break from the worms and snot and raw fucking hopelessness that were oozing out of me and asked him where we go from here.

The first year was the toughest. Some days I would walk down that hall into a meeting as Superwoman. More often I was rolling down the same hall spread-eagle on a wheel of death, naked, glimpsing wide-eyed boys watching me crash into walls and chairs.

Everyone goes through it differently; I heard that a lot. Even so, can you tell me how they got through it differently? The German aunts weren't talking, and my peers were *my* age, too young for menopause.

It was difficult to leave the house some days. But I did it; we do it. Out of nowhere appeared a sane twin who watched over me, kept me from killing anyone.

* * *

Three years later I was working out of my home office, expecting a client. She called, crying, to say she wouldn't be keeping her appointment. She had just left to meet with me when her car broke down in the middle of a busy intersection. She got out of the car, walked to the front bumper, and repeatedly kicked it. Then she turned and walked home.

"No worries," I said. "We'll reschedule when you feel better."

MY BIG FAT GAY MARRIAGE ISSUE, RESOLVED

BRYN DOUGLAS MARLOW

The minister signed our marriage certificate with a flourish, then said, "One of you needs to sign here as 'husband' and one over here as 'wife.'" It was 2005. Dave and I were wed in Canada on our ninth anniversary as a couple, soon after Ontario legalized same-sex marriage—so soon that gender-neutral forms were not yet available.

When we returned to the U.S., our marital status lodged in the Twilight Zone. It's still there. We believe we're married. A whole vast country north of us believes we're married. But what happens in Canada stays in Canada. According to those with saying power, Dave is married to nobody. Guess what that makes me.

Being nobody wears on a person. Researchers have long documented the negative effects of the stigma of homosexuality on gay people. Recent studies show that residing in a U.S. state that outlaws same-sex marriage has a direct, adverse effect on the mental health of lesbians and gay men.

It makes me sick to live in Indiana in a marital state of perpetual confusion. Here's my marital history: Not married, twenty-three years. Married, fourteen years. Not married, seven years. Married, but not according to my state or federal government, nine years. Married and recognized as such by the state, thirty-six hours. Back to married-but-not-married, two months, followed by ten days of being married. Then back to yes-but-no, then over to yes-but-not-really, not until the Supreme Court says it's okay. (Did you follow that?)

In June, a federal judge ruled Indiana's same-sex marriage ban unconstitutional. As gay couples lined up to obtain marriage licenses, Dave and I marveled. We could sip coffee at our own kitchen table as a *bona fide* married couple. For all of three days. The court ruling was stayed, pending appeal. For us, it was back to life in limbo.

Our summer vacation offered a breath of fresh air. We spent ten consecutive days touring several states and two provinces where marriage equality is the law of the land. "This is the longest we've been married since we got hitched," Dave said.

Toward the end of our trip we visited Niagara Falls and took in the view from the Canadian side, along with a thousand or more other spectators. So much water rushing over the brink made me have to pee. When I returned from the restroom I soon spotted Dave among the crowd. It's not all that difficult to recognize someone you care about.

At the same time it's easy to dismiss those you refuse to see. Experience has taught me this. My three children have severed contact with me over my coming out as gay. As has my brother. As have former friends and fellow church members. No place at the table for the likes of me.

Where am I welcome? Life keeps me guessing. This past weekend I attended a college class reunion. I almost didn't show up. I often encounter judgment and rejection from people who knew me before I came out of the closet. I feared more of the same should my classmates learn I am gay. I tested the waters. The first time a fellow alumnus asked about my spouse, I mentioned Dave by name. I was peppered with questions, taken to task for believing homosexuality cannot be changed, and charged with a lack of religious faith. *Sheesh.* Thereafter I mostly dodged questions about marriage and family. I avoided some conversations altogether. I shut down, hung back, withdrew. I was present but not present—off in limbo land again. This is familiar territory; I check in there frequently to visit my marital status.

As you know, the federal court of appeals ruled against Indiana's gay marriage ban. The state has appealed to the U.S. Supreme Court. But I've been thinking: Dave and I could settle the matter now. As our state government is so antsy about keeping marriage between a husband and wife, we should send the folks in Indianapolis a copy of our Canadian marriage license. It's there in black and white: on March 12, 2005, Dave took me to be his lawfully wedded wife.

IN THIS PLACE

BARBARA DAVIS

I stepped into a long, low building at the Nazi death camp, Majdanek. Near the door a weathered wooden sign said, "Bad und Desinfektion." At the other end of the building was a chimney.

A few steps inside the gas chamber was a cement swimming pool for children to play in while the adults got undressed for their showers. The showerheads were still in place. At the very last moment, the children were gathered up and thrown like footballs over the heads of their parents and the door slammed shut. There was a gas-proof peephole on the door where SS men stood and watched for the 18 or so minutes it took everyone to die. The glass on the peephole had been smashed.

After the killing, forced laborers began the task of separating the bodies, putting them on carts, and sending them to the dissection room to be searched for gold teeth and jewelry. The walls and ceiling of the huge room bore sea-blue stains from the Zyklon B gas. Two carbon monoxide tanks were bolted to the wall in one corner, and hundreds of metal Zyklon B canisters, still full of pellets, stood in tall stacks behind chain link on the other side of the room.

My eyes stung in this place, my lungs clenched like fists. I grabbed at a wooden beam in the middle of the room and closed my eyes. When I realized that thousands of people had clung to this very beam while sucking their last breaths, I didn't jump back but held the beam even tighter.

"I'm here," I told them. "I feel you. I will tell what I've seen."

This was Christmas Eve, 2005.

My sister and I had tormented ourselves about whether or not to go to Poland for several months. She felt great trepidation about jumping into such a dark and surreal situation—a ten-day tour of *nine* Nazi concentration and death camps—as her introduction to human rights activism. She had been invited onto the tour by a fellow professor who specialized in human rights. She invited me to come along for moral support. Both of us cringed at the names of some of the camps on the itinerary: Treblinka, Sobibor, Auschwitz, Birkenau. But, it seemed this was a once-in-a-lifetime opportunity. As the summer months changed into fall, we decided to go.

From December 18 through December 28, 2005, we rode trains and vans and buses at top speed through Poland, the madness of one camp building on the next, with only Christmas Day off to rest.

After landing in Warsaw, we took a long train ride up to Gdansk and from there visited the concentration camp Stutthof. The barracks were preserved, with exhibits including the striped uniforms and wooden clogs worn by inmates who had been shipped in from the occupied countries of Western Europe. One of the uniforms had a pink upside-down triangle over the left breast. A homosexual. While the other members of the tour remained in the exhibits, I walked alone on a long road to the back of the camp, where a tiny brick gas chamber stood with the crematorium nearby. Next to the exit of the gas chamber were a huge wooden Star of David and a Christian cross. Behind these an old cattle car, used to transport the prisoners, sat on a section of tracks. It looked barely tall enough to stand up in.

I went into the crematorium, where wreaths of plastic flowers sat in the mouths of the ovens. Each oven had a metal slab inside it, onto which a body would be placed to burn. I reached into one of the ovens and touched the wooden handle of the slab. I was here, really here. This was no black and white documentary. Someone had been gassed or worked to death and burned on this slab. A student from the tour came inside the crematorium and I yanked my hand away, fearing I had desecrated this place by touching it. Maybe I had.

Our next camp was the death camp Chelmno. Here the old and infirm, the mentally unstable, the Poles and Jews and Gypsies of the region, and many thousands of Soviet POWs had been loaded into huge vans converted into gas chambers and then driven, suffocating, the 2.5 miles to their own burial pits in the woods. Witnesses had heard screaming as the vans passed. We drove the exact route the vans had taken, from the old manor where the prisoners had undressed and left their belongings to the forest camp, which now consisted of nothing more than mass graves in a huge clearing in the woods.

Each grave measured approximately 280 yards long by 20 feet wide, and there were enough of them to hold 340,000 bodies. I could see outlines of the graves in the deep snow. I dug a few inches down until I found beautiful black marble that delineated the edges of the grave. Its gold flecks shone in the sunlight, which warmed and calmed me through a huge down coat and gloves and arctic snow boots. It was strange, but I could breathe here.

Similarly, at Treblinka, where an estimated 1.2 million people evaporated, the camp suddenly took on the appearance of a landscape out of Narnia. This was to become a recurring, uncomfortable sensation in Poland—the grievous history of the camps versus the incredible beauty of that particular winter, with snow bending the great forests and sparkling in the sunlight and against the brilliant blue of the skies. Later, my sister told me she doesn't remember the brutality of Treblinka, but the magic—a place she often returns to in her mind to experience eternity.

Every time I hear a certain car company lauding "the power of German engineering" on TV, my stomach does a flip and I remember the indoor railroad track leading from the gas chamber to the crematorium at Auschwitz. When I saw the cart for bodies on a railroad track—a railroad track *inside* the gas chamber—I thought I would throw up. Of all the death machinery I had witnessed on this tour, this indoor railroad track brought into shocking focus the incredible swiftness and ingenuity with which the Nazis dispatched their victims. I covered my mouth with my hand, paid quick respects at the crematorium, and then fled the building.

At Birkenau, I climbed the steps of the famous elevated train station whose image so often shows up in Holocaust documentaries. From up inside the station, you can see the train tracks stretch the full length of the immense camp, which was built to receive 100,000 forced laborers and exterminate millions of Jews. About halfway down, the tracks split; one line goes to the selection platform, the other straight back to the blown-up ruins of the gas chambers and crematoria. I walked the tracks alone, picked up a rock, put it back down. Around the ruins the ground was soft and spongy underfoot—ashes—all that is left of the 1.5 million people who perished at that place, the site of the greatest massacre in human history.

Incredibly, a blue enamel mug sat in plain sight on one of the ruins. I picked it up and checked inside—it was rotted through, a real relic from the Holocaust. Had some SS officer sipped his coffee from that mug while looking through the peephole of the gas chamber? I didn't know what to do with it. For a moment, I wanted to hide it inside my coat and take it home with me. Then, horrified at myself, I tossed it back onto the ruins. It dropped between the bricks and vanished from view. This was my last experience at a Nazi death camp. I had seen enough.

The day we left Poland, we stopped at Oskar Schindler's factory in Krakow. The guards let us slip inside the gates, though the museum was not yet open to the public. They showed us the steep staircase that appears in *Schindler's List*, and let us go up the stairs to Schindler's office. Inside, his original furnishings remained. I kissed his desk. The guards led us to a pile of rubble from recent renovations and told us we could fill our pockets with tiles and anything else we found. While the rest of the tour went inside the concentration camp where Schindler's workers had lived, I stayed on the bus and fingered my jagged pieces of tile.

I cried on and off for a month after the long flight home from Warsaw. I winced at the sight of old brick chimneys. I read every book on the Holocaust I could get my hands on and it still didn't begin to make sense to me. Nine years later, I am still nauseated by the crash course in hatred I took in the winter of 2005. I will never fully understand what I saw. But I do understand that the camps in Poland must remain intact to tell their story so that it never happens again.

INTERVIEW

DEANNA MORRIS INTERVIEWS CHRISTOPHER COAKE

"No one else alive had known him like they had; no one could return that faint submarine ping."

- *You Came Back* by Christopher Coake.

Mark, the protagonist of the novel, speaking about his ex-wife and deceased son, voices an achingly beautiful truth of what it means to be really known by someone else. The ninety-minute interview I did with Christopher Coake cannot begin to "return the ping," but hopefully begins a reader's process of knowing him. Chris, as he prefers to be called, describes his writing as "entering into conversation." He and I entered into conversation at the Indiana Writers Center *Gathering of Writers* event on Saturday, November 16, 2013, where he was featured as the keynote speaker.

I began by asking Chris what it felt like to be named by *Granta* as one of the twenty best young American novelists, a publication that has published such literary greats as Raymond Carver, Tobias Wolff, and Sylvia Plath. "Pants-wetting terrifying," he answered. He smiled as he said it. He explained the three-day wait to find out exactly why *Granta* had contacted him (after exchanging voicemails and emails) as an anxious time. "I thought they just wanted me to submit a story, but I wasn't sure." As we know now, they were notifying him of his selection as one of the twenty best. They also requested a new short story to appear in the issue. "I felt I had to write a story that would hit it out of the park because I was on the twenty best list." He was under pressure, as all writers are at times, but he emphasized, "I love this writing life, even with all the anxiety. It is a good problem to have."

I reminded him of a quote about *Granta* made by *The Observer* that *Granta* "has its face pressed firmly against the window, determined to witness the world." I asked Chris if he feels, as a writer, that he has his "face pressed firmly against the window, determined to witness the world?" He answered with a quick and definitive, "No." He sees his role, "perhaps like many other authors," to be writing with a sense of locality, even when addressing universal issues, adding that "each author has his or her own cultural and personal references." Chris recognizes that his particular references, among others, are grief and loneliness. He continued that many American writers are just that—American writers, American-centric. He suggests that American authors can speak well to the theme of isolation, but with America becoming more and more integrated into the global community, there may be a need, and desire, to write from a broader viewpoint. (Chris has not traveled in any extensive way, but his novel has been translated into German, French, and

Italian.) He laughed quietly and said, "Maybe I will write the Great American novel, though. Then again, maybe it is not relevant or necessary to do so." It seemed he was debating the idea as he spoke.

I almost whispered my next question about his themes of death in both his novel *You Came Back* and short story collection *We're In Trouble Now.* I prefaced my question with "Chris, you approach the theme of death with respect and tenderness. I understand that your first wife died at an early age. How did you come to the place where you were able to write about the topic of death?" He answered, "It was difficult, but I needed to write about it and about the prospect of someone living without hope, within the boundaries of a finite life. It was many years before I was able to write about it. I wanted to open up questions about what love is, what happens when the rational meets the irrational."

I changed the subject for a moment and asked him what three things, besides his computer, are on his writing desk. "A coffee cup with a lid and I don't know what's inside of it, a Tylenol bottle because of a bicycle whiplash, and audio speakers to listen to music without lyrics, heavy metal." The topic of heavy metal music segued into the next question.

"Who is the most intriguing person you have ever met?" He named more than one. "Thurston Moore of Sonic Youth (the heavy metal band). Also, the cast from *Mystery Science Theater* who visited campus. And a friend of his who is a magician." We all "make art in different ways." His students intrigue him and influence him as well. Chris describes himself as a "lawful guy." The students hold him accountable to his own writing rules (laws). "They also keep my ego in check." He loves the university life because a university is a place "where we are making things and making things better."

He wrote most of his latest book on campus, late into the night. Picture this: he sits in his university office, alone, Chris the only person in the building (even the cleaning crew is finished for the night) writing a story with strong themes of grief and ghosts. When it is time for him to return to his car and head home, he has to pass a campus memorial, a homage to a murdered policeman. It's after midnight, it's dark, Chris is alone, and his characters are his only company. He said he "jogged quickly past the memorial each night." And he doesn't even believe in ghosts.

The storyline of the deceased son as a ghost prompted my next question. I quoted science fiction writer David Brin, who said, "If you have other things in your life— family, friends, good productive day of work—these can interact with your writing and the sum will be all the richer."

My question was twofold:

Is *You Came Back* ever categorized as science fiction? What are the other things in your life?

Chris replied that usually his book is described as "literary fiction." Occasionally it may be described as "horror" but it does not fit that genre, nor does it fit in science fiction. "Bookstores need to know where to place your book." The conversation turned to the idea of bookstores and electronic books and self-publishing. (We do come back to the topic of other things in his life.)

He says that "bookstores curate; electronic book distribution does not." There is a sense of old school versus new and that Chris embraces progress, but he is firmly loyal to the traditional publishing route. "Until it's not there any longer, I will continue to publish through established publishing houses." I asked him if the marketing side of the writing business is better handled by publishers than the authors themselves? "I don't have a marketing bone in my body, so yes, for me it is." He is happy to speak at conferences and be interviewed, however. He knows writers who have "platforms" and push their work, but that is not his style.

Now, for the "other things in his life." Teaching at the University of Nevada is a large part of his life, and Chris has remarried and has two dogs. He showed me a picture of his dog, named Dashiell Hammett, a mix of German Shepherd and Beagle, who loves veggie smoothies, cocks his head when listening to humans, and responds to the names of his dog toys. One toy in particular is a football that the family calls "fumble." One of the other things in Chris's life is football, and Dashiell watches it with him. When the referee calls "fumble," Dashiell retrieves his toy "fumble." The enjoyment Chris derives from his pets is obvious as he speaks about them. "Dogs keep you humble and in the moment." The other dog, Kona, is a black lab rescue dog and "ate their green couch."

Chris has a new novel in the works. I asked him to tell me about it. Because it is currently a work in progress, he says that the book may turn out differently than he describes now. It is somewhat violent in theme and explores a vast period of time of the main character, ages sixteen to forty. About an Indiana boy who ends up on a Nevada political compound, the story is "action packed" and "told from several characters' perspectives."

Our conversation returned to his recent book *You Came Back*. There is a cultural reference in the book about the day of 9-11. He wanted to frame his character's grief "in the context of national grief." Much of what the character experiences, our nation experienced. His personal grief, the character's grief, can seem too self-centered otherwise. "Grief is not exclusive." The day after the towers were hit, his professor said, "Art still matters, I think." Perhaps that is another reason Chris included the event in the story.

I mentioned to Chris that each page of his novel contains poignant lines, including even his "Acknowledgments" page. It reads, in part, "If you would like to imagine the author of this book as a solitary fellow, working alone and friendless, please close the book now." With the exception of the late nights at his campus office! The acknowledgments are generous and comprehensive.

The interview was coming to a close, so I asked him for what I call a Coake quote. "No means go to work on it." A rejection of a written piece means "it's not ready yet" and the writer must "persevere through criticism."

There is a simple, elegant line in *You Came Back*. It is spoken by the character Allie, girlfriend to Mark. "Allie loved playing make-believe." The line is perfectly fitting (on many levels) for the scene, a woman dealing with life by pretending. Perhaps, too, writing—that pretending through fiction—allows the writer (and the reader) to face reality. Chris does "not believe in ghosts" but by "playing make-believe" in his fiction, he confronts the matters that haunt. His writing will take you there.

CHRISTOPHER COAKE is the author of the novel *You Came Back* (2012) and the collection of short stories *We're in Trouble* (2005), which won the PEN/Robert Bingham Fellowship. In addition, Coake was listed among *Granta*'s "Best of Young American Novelists" in 2007. His stories have been published in several literary journals and anthologized in *Best American Noir of the Century*. A native Hoosier, he received his MFA in fiction. Born and raised in Indiana, he was the 2012 recipient of the Eugene and Marilyn Glick Indiana Regional Author Award.

A member of the Indiana Writers Center, Deanna Morris holds an MFA from Butler University. She has published stories, poems, and articles in numerous places.

AUTHOR BIOGRAPHIES

DAN CARPENTER is an Indianapolis resident, freelance writer, and contributor to *Indianapolis Business Journal, StatehouseFile.Com,* and other publications. He has published poems in *Poetry East, Illuminations, Pearl, Xavier Review, Southern Indiana Review, Maize, Tipton Poetry Journal, Flying Island,* and other journals. A book of his poems, *More Than I Could See,* was published in 2009 by Restoration Press. One of his poems was included in *And Know This Place* (Indiana Historical Society Press, 2011), the first comprehensive anthology of work by Indiana-connected poets.

Originally from San Diego, and a CPA by profession, TERI COSTELLO took down her shingle in 2011 and moved to Indianapolis after living in Los Angeles and Chicago. In her words, "Life now is sweet, close, and personal."

BARBARA DAVIS is at work on her first novel. She holds a Bachelor's degree in Social Sciences from Harvard University and a Master's in US History from the University of Colorado, Boulder. She lives in Indianapolis with her 18 year-old son.

JAMES FIGY is a writer from Indianapolis. He has two cats, two rabbits, a coffee dependency, an amateurish collection of Duke Ellington LPs, and a degree in creative writing from the University of Indianapolis. His creative work has appeared in *Flying Island, Punchnel's,* and UIndy's student literary journal *Etchings.*

LESLIE LYNNTON FULLER is an Indianapolis-based writer.

ANNE HAINES's chapbook, *Breach*, was published by Finishing Line Press in 2008. Individual poems have appeared in *Diode, Field, New Madrid, Rattleiz, Tipton Poetry Journal*, the anthology *And Know This Place: Poetry of Indiana*, and elsewhere. She lives in Bloomington, where she works as the Web Content Specialist for the Indiana University Libraries. She can be found online at http://annehaines.wordpress.com and on Twitter at @annehaines.

JENNIFER HURLEY received an MA in Liberal Studies, Concentration: English, from Valparaiso University. She currently teaches English at Valparaiso High School. Her poetry, fiction, and essays have appeared in various literary publications, including *The Cresset, Etchings, Plath Profiles* (multiple issues), and *Valparaiso Poetry Review*.

GEORGE KALAMARAS, Indiana State Poet Laureate, is the author of seven books of poetry and seven chapbooks, including *Kingdom of Throat-Stuck Luck*, winner of the Elixir Press Poetry Prize (2011). He is a Professor of English at Indiana University-Purdue University Fort Wayne, where he has taught since 1990.

CRYSTAL LYNN KAMM is a professional writer and a daydreamer. She writes web pages by day and fiction by night, and somewhere in between she finds time to enjoy reading and hiking with her husband and red golden retriever.

NORBERT KRAPF, Indiana State Poet Laureate 2008-2010, is the author of ten full-length poetry collections, the latest being *American Dreams: Reveries and Reflections* (2013) and *Songs in Sepia and Black and White* (2012). In April 2014, his *Catholic Boy Blues: A Poet's Journal of Healing* appeared. He has collaborated with jazz pianist Monika Herzig, with whom he released a CD, *Imagine*, and with bluesman Gordon Bonham. He has also collaborated with photographers Daryl Jones, David Pierini, and Richard Fields in books published by Indiana University Press.

ROBIN LOVELACE was born and raised in Indianapolis, lived in Evansville for a few years, and now lives in Plainfield with her husband and her dog. She has been writing stories on and off for at least thirty years. Three short stories were published in various literary magazines in the 1990s, and she won second place in the Ohio Valley Fiction Contest in 2000. Her novel *Secret Ravens: A Fountain Square Story* was published in October 2013. Robin is currently working on a science fiction story set in Memphis.

JAYNE MAREK's poetry has appeared in publications such as *Lantern Journal, Siren, Spillway, Driftwood Bay, Tipton Poetry Journal, Isthmus, The Occasional Reader, Wisconsin Academy Review, Windless Orchard*, and several anthologies. In 2013, Finishing Line Press published her first chapbook, and Chatter House Press brought out a book of poems she co-authored with Lylanne Musselman and Mary Sexson.

Chickens and other fowl pursuits occupy BRYN DOUGLAS MARLOW (gayfeather.wordpress.com) on a wooded 1930s farmstead in east central Indiana. His creative nonfiction and personal essays, like this present one (with a nod to Brian Doyle), have appeared in *The Sun, Utne Reader, White Crane Journal*, and *RFD*, among others. His first published work of fiction appeared in *Flying Island* in 2014.

TRACY MISHKIN is a career immigrant. Born in academia, she taught in Georgia and published two books on African American literature, then disappeared, resurfacing in the land of non-profits with the Bureau of Jewish Education in Indianapolis. Three years later, she was spotted across the border working retail at the Uniform House before she immigrated to the corporate world, where she resolves insurance problems at Anthem Blue Cross Blue Shield. Finishing Line Press published her chapbook *I Almost Didn't Make It to McDonald's* in 2014. Her work has appeared in *Reckless Writing Poetry Anthology* 2013, *Tipton Poetry Journal, Flying Island, Poetica*, and in the Focus 9-11 section of PoetsUSA.com.

LYLANNE MUSSELMAN is a native Hoosier with many family, friendship, and poetry ties that keep her returning often. An award-winning artist and poet, she has been published in many literary journals and anthologies. She's authored three chapbooks and co-authored *Company of Women: New and Selected Poems* (Chatter House Press, 2013) with Jayne Marek and Mary Sexson. Although in 2011, she moved to Toledo, Ohio, she continues teaching online writing classes for Ivy Tech Community College, Indianapolis.

MAUREEN O'HERN is a former English teacher, a botanical artist, a graduate of Purdue University and a member of the Indiana Writers Center.

THOMAS ALAN ORR's poems have appeared in *Good Poems*, edited by Garrison Keillor, and other anthologies and journals. His poetry has also been read into the record of the Maine State Legislature. His first book of poems was *Hammers in the Fog*. He is finishing a second book under the working title *Tongue to the Anvil*.

JEFFREY OWEN PEARSON's poems appear in *So It Goes*, *Reckless Writing Anthology*, *Tipton Poetry Journal*, *Flying Island*, and *Maize*. His chapbook *Hawaii Slides* was published by Pudding House Publications. A member of the Midwest Writers Workshop, he lives in Muncie.

RICHARD PFLUM is a native of, and now lives in, Indianapolis. He is the author of three full-length books of poetry, *A Dream of Salt* (The Fredrick Brewer Press, now The Raintree Press, 1980), *A Strange Juxtaposition of Parts* (The Writers' Center Press, 1995), and *Some Poems to Be Read Out Loud* (Chatter House Press, 2013). He has appeared in *Tears in the Fence* (U.K.), *Flying Island*, *The Reaper*, *Exquisite Corpse*, *PlopLop*, *Hopewell Review*, and *Kayak*. He also has poems in the anthologies *The Indiana Experience* (Indiana University Press, 1977) and *A New Geography of Poets* (University of Arkansas Press, 1992), two poems in *The New Laurel Review* (1999), and a poem in *Glass Works* (Pudding House, 2002). On the Internet, he can be found on the archive PoetryNet, Poet of the Month, October 2003. He is the host of *Evening With the Muse*, a monthly reading and open mic of the Indiana Writers Center.

STEPHEN R. ROBERTS lives on eight acres of Hoosier soil, pretending it to be wilderness. He spends more time now with grandchildren, trees, and poetry, not necessarily in that order. It is the love of these things, along with lariats and other fine examples of rope, that keeps him tying up words, knotting or unknotting poems.

MARY SEXSON is the author of the book *103 in the Light, Selected Poems 1996-2000* (Restoration Press, 2004), nominated for a Best Books of Indiana award in 2005. She is the co-author of *Company of Women, New and Selected Poems* (Chatter House Press, 2013) with Jayne Marek and Lylanne Musselman. Her poems have appeared in various literary publications, and her newer work is included in several anthologies, including *The Globetrotter's Companion* (Lion Lounge Press, London, 2011), *A Few Good Words* (Cincinnati Writer's Project, 2013), and the online site *New Verse News* (2013). She has forthcoming work in *Reckless Writing Anthology* (Chatter House Press).

JO BARBARA TAYLOR lives outside of Raleigh, North Carolina, grew up in Indiana and remains an Indiana farm girl at heart. She taught English in public school for twenty-one years. Her poems and academic writing have appeared in journals, including *Tipton Poetry Journal* and *Inwood Indiana*, magazines, and anthologies. She leads poetry workshops for the North Carolina Poetry Society and Osher Lifelong Learning Institute through Duke Continuing Education. She has published four chapbooks, the most recent, *High Ground* by Main Street Rag, 2013.

HELEN TOWNSEND lives in Indianapolis. "One of my favorite things is sitting down to write or revise, and when I look at the clock, hours have gone by. Everyone who writes or makes art or has a great conversation has experienced that. It feels like a glimpse of eternity."

RANDALL WIREMAN received a Bachelor of Science in Biology from Purdue University. By day, Randy is the technical advisor for a pharmaceutical industry service provider who spends his lunch periods editing the chapters and stories that fiction writer Randy has created the previous night. While the two Randys have had some sharp differences, both have successfully collaborated in writing gay technical protocols inspiring love and fiction romance involving assays and high throughput screening. Wait. Reverse that.

ACKNOWLEDGMENTS

The Indiana Writers Center gratefully acknowledges the support of these individuals:

Editors
Executive Editor, Barbara Shoup
Managing and Fiction Editor, David Hassler
Creative Nonfiction Editor, Julianna Thibodeaux
Poetry Editor, J.L. Kato

Copyeditors
Michael Baumann
Andrea Boucher

Book Design and Layout, Michael Baumann

Cover Design, Andrea and Anna Boucher

Cover Photo, Dragan Maric

Individual Donors
Anonymous
Debra Horberg
Dwayne Isaacs
Michael Johnson
Sonja Kantor
Lori Schankerman
Harry Todd
Eleanor Vonnegut

www.ingramcontent.com/pod-product-compliance
Lightning Source LLC
Chambersburg PA
CBHW070639130626
46555CB00006B/2622